WITH HER AGAIN

A SCI-FI ROMANCE

LOUIS KAEY

Made with ♥ on the Notion Press Platform
www.notionpress.com

To

that little fun girl

who partnered my inner spark

to lava out the clean slate thing called

LOVE.

Contents

CHAPTER I

Planting a feet on the glassy road shining with slippery radiant colours was meant to be a sin. Calvry, after the 9 minutes travel over the 50 kilometres committed such a sin with no regret but as the negligence. The lazy deranged face of him shown out his wonderfully ruined day. The first time when he headed up his eyes towards sky scrappers, one of them boldly displayed the commercial for the new-to-market electro-magnetic bike- the racy ship. He sighed in great disapproval and walked about to the north of that scrapper. The analog piece clinging to his hand which meant to be crushed or museumed gave a sleepy hourly ring. The hands touching at 4'O. Eight hours to the regeneration of the year- 2090.

Calvry slithered among the people like a well-fueled space shuttle even in his 90's.The phone in his pocket began to blare. He took that out and put it back after giving a rushed view on the screen and sped.His shoulders ditched smoothly with few other rushers like him. But he never lucked them an apology. After all, the opposite party even didn't noticed it. After couple of minutes of snake run he slowed down near one of the sky scrapper grown like a giant about to eat children.

The sky scrapper has bathed itself with reflective single-sided mirrors, most of them were made into screens to display commercials,which reflected the clear blue sky and wooly clouds as if they've brought them down to the earth, for now. Calvry stood before the magnificent glass shield disguised as door. The entry. His forehead pricked out few beads of fancy moist points, not runny. The glass shield hissed open, flushing a swirl of breeze on his face, scanning him completely and based on the consumed data from his retina. **WELCOME TO CROSS' MEMORIES,**a screechy robotic invitation had anytime been his core hatred. The interior smelled like a strawberry dipped in wine and bitten partly while Calvry's being not-so-great fan of strawberry.

The lady at the counter 6- mid-twenties, silky black hair, small, blunt yet fit-to-face nose- called and spelled out his name with an all-day-good-day smile. That makes a pro.

'Welcome to cross' memories,sir. You are under the consultation of DOT52. Let's tick your data first,'she smiled again, bowing her eyes to the 10 inch or so sized flat screen. 'You are Calvry. 92 years. height 5'8. Married...' The clearance went for a minute and got turned in with '... No time travel license and published several articles against our Mr.Cross.'

'I'm a journalist,'he volunteered.

'I can crystally see that, sir. For now, you are under the category of our threat,'she closed the screen, 'Could you clear your purpose of being here, sir?'

'I wanted to meet Mr.Cross. A friendly visit.'

'It's not possible. I can't allow you to have him as you're sensed as a threat to this place and to Mr.Cross,'she said with a steal face.

The next moment, an earpiece sticking to her left year singled a sound. She pressed it firmly to receive the call or kind of. And, after few *YES SIRs,* the call went terminated. She put that mechanical smile to her face again. 'Mr.Cross would like to see you, sir. Follow me, please.'

She took him to the elevator and number 31 was pressed among the strip of buttons. Calvry had been here to this place and even to the 31st floor like numerous times with his colleagues to run interviews.And, few times with

Mr.Cross himself as they're school buddies otherwise than the business. But this was his first time to be here alone. That, forced him to take all the normal proceedings.

The corridor of 31st floor reverberated their steps. It was shiny, modern, highly recent but empty as anything. Calvry felt like walking into a grey sky or giant AC vent. DOT52 paced in front of him with steady speed, not turning back onto him. The end of the corridor was made up so dramatically with a silver painted door, no seats but with a bunch of fake lavender flowers bowled in mismatch. While he was sarcastically praising the taste of Mr.Cross, DOT52 scanned her retina which served as the key. The door unlocked.

'It's a scary surprise to see you alone here, my friend.' Mr.Cross hugged him warmly.

'Thank you, Cross,' he received with a partial face, escaping him from the hug.

'What's up strict pen? you need another interview? a secret interview about my formula and how I come to consume my time travel machines? shoot me. It's my pleasure to have your bullet at my chest,'he winked.

'I need a favour from you, Cross,' he almost whispered.

'That's engrossing. Go on,' he planted his eyes onto his.

'I mean I need it to be served in personal.'

Calvry took a indicative quick glance at DOT52. She was there generally 5 steps behind him staring at them.

'Don't mind about her,' he laughed, 'DOT52. Go to sleep.'

'Command received,' she replied with her shrill voice and fell dead on the ground.

'Oh my...' Calvry widened his eyes. Mr.Cross laughed again. A long maddening ghostly laughter.

‘Don’t pee, Calv. It’s a humanoid. Trusting a human is like packing venom for dinner, isn’t it? Unlike they’re you. A Strong, naive, life-giver. Now, try me.’

‘Before that I want you to forget about everything that was staging and about to stage. Deal?’

‘It’s not. I can’t force a lie. I’m not going to forget it. Again human. But I can give you an assurance of vaulting it.‘

’I’d appreciate that,‘ he mumbled and cleared his voice,’ I wanted to travel back in time with your machine.‘

’Stupidly uncanny. I mean according to you. But,why do you wanted to use mine while all the economic and commercial centers stands one for no cost?‘ he bridged his brows.

’Two reasons. First, I don’t have a license. Then, I’d never love to be watched by the people who read my articles negative to it.‘ a seriously begging tone.

’Second one can be taken,‘ He grinned.

’Whatever. Could you do that for me?‘

’Yes. I can. But I‘m little puzzled about your request-

’Favour. Not a request. You can say no and walk me out,‘he burned.

’Ok. A favour. Why after these many years?‘

’Your favour requires that?‘

’Calv, we are into something illegal. If we are caught, we are done. So, I need to know,‘ he charmed the sheep.

Calvry sighed and put his face to the feet.

’I mean to propose a girl from my past. Don’t come again with another WH- question.‘

Calvry picked up his face at snail pace to witness the comical mocking expression of Mr.Cross.

’No. I‘m not,’he said swallowing his burst out.

CHAPTER II

DOT52 lied on the floor influenced by Mr.Cross' command. Calvry glanced at her like handful of times and discomfited Mr.Cross.The room was engaged in filling itself with the aroma of coffee which spirited up from the disposal mug placed before Mr.Cross and Calvry. The last sun of the year, blanketed into the orange wool of clouds was visible clearly behind Mr.Cross' head. Calvry watched it like a movie.The Cold stay between them got never tilted even after emptying half a mug of their coffee.

'Are we doing this? I'm scared of your unspoken' Calvry broke the ice.

Mr.Cross cleared his voice. 'See Calv. There's nothing new I'm going to say to you now. As you're writing me about for years, you must be wholly aware of the restrictions and policies of my machine.'

'Yes. I do,'he confirmed.

'So, I have mentioned in thousands of interview, the core purpose to invent my time machine is to revisit the memories and to have them much friendly without altering them. And, today it helps in crime clearance, taking reference for the future maintenance and for people to revisit their missed one's charming days.'

Calvry sat there paralyzed.

'That's the reason for our training of three courses, almost an year prior to the license offer. The machine itself scan the scene from your unconscious brain based on the time and date you have entered before you could use them. So that, in any case,if you try to alter the past, the machine alarms the police and you'll be killed out their and you'd have left to lead your life from the place you die.'

'That's my commotion against your machines. The idea even have a concept of manslaughter and punishing it with a loop in time. But, I need to hoist this now,' he maintained his line.

'Sorry Calv. I can't allow you. If you are going to nail a proposal that you hadn't done before, then it's a fate switch. Get that? I can't risk your life and the real future.' Mr.Cross sipped his last chilled drop of his bored coffee, 'DOT52. Rise and shine.' She was up like a new born lady, the very next snap.

'Thank you, Cross,'he pushed the chair to leave.

'Umm...Wait, Calv,' he grinned,'you see I can't take you to your past to your so called hearty crush. But,your task is hugely magnetive. I love that. Who would like to go back in time to propose a girl at the age of damn ninety-five?'

'Ninety-two,' he corrected.

'Yeah. As you wish. Ninety-two. That's captivating, right? So, I have other option for you. Only by your ground of dare.'

Calvry leaned to the table.

'Right-O,' Mr.Cross continued,'It is still under progress. Not yet even named. But a weird and much safer baby than the Time machine.'

'Tell me about it,' he interested.

'I could show you,' he smiled and turned around near DOT52, 'Down, now. I can take this from here.'

He whispered in her ear.

'Command received.' Again the same shrill.

After her departure, Mr.Cross approached the cool brown-shaded wall to his left corner. That's when Calvry noticed the slim aperture in the wall which slid side wise into a compact three person compartment.

'Come in, Calv,' he waved him an invitation. But his face showering a quirky unassuming expression.

Calvry walked in like he was hypnotized. It's an elevator, he noticed the strip of call buttons. But the arrangement in the buttons was little difference than the before. zero, then minus one to minus four.That's the punch. Mr.Cross pressed on minus three and locked the elevator.

Travel in that elevator became Calvry's swift move of life time. It trailed down like it was unwired and hit the floor with the gentle shake. Mr.Cross unlocked the elevator into the room of jammed cable cabinets. It looked as if they're entering into the libraray of on-usage electronic trash. A fresh fear and a delocating clutch at the guts saved Calvry silent through the walk. To the meeting point of his enabled sight Calvry saw a huge desk married with a metal seat, oddly cushioned. On the table, there was an unrecognizable helmet like thing sitting dead thing reminding him of classic slasher movies.

'Hold my new baby,' Mr.Cross passed the helmet like thing technically linked with cables with a transparent display over the top, to Calvry.

'What in the world am I holding Cross?'he said childishly.

'I told you, it's not named yet. But, I can explain you that,'he brought back the helmet to the desk and asked him to sit there while he butted on the desk.

Calvry prepared himself geniunely for the lecture.

'It's a simple fantasy yet complicated for believing. Let's consider, Calvry, that means you are X and an arbitrary person is Y. The possibility for the coincidence of being perpendicular between this X and Y are highly positive, normally. But in our case this Y is not even Y. It is X+.'

'What?which means?,' Calvry demanded.

'Which means this X and X+ have to lead a same life. Go through same scenarios. Meeting someone like exactly under same circumstances, so on.'

'Is that really a theory or you simply trying to pull my leg,' he smirked.

'Why should I? Hell, it happens under parallel life theory.'

'How that going to assist me?'

'Hold on.We're not yet done. Right-O. Let me put you through a question. What if I swap your mind with your thoughts, ideas and dreams into the foreign one. That is X+?'

'Mess. A greater explosion. A suicidal attempt,' Calvry replied.

'Damn right. Now, consider this X+ we are talking about is X himself. That means two Calvrys with exactly everything fits, living a same life without an inch bounce.'

'So, you are prescribing to find such a photocopy or clone of me to switch my mind so that I can propose my far away crush. Right? That's damn stupid too,'he busted.

'Ahan. Here comes the difference between the nuanced science man and an imaginative story teller. I can do as you said but I have to find many Xs, then. Your crush, your mother,another Mr.Cross so on. We can chase one but it can't created. Initiating to my final point, these parallel personalities and the incidents could be viable in one place as per your comment.'

'Where,then?' he said passively.

'In the other universe. A parallel universe. All things that happens in this earth can happen there too. Your girl will be there at the same place and time you wanted her to be.It's much more handy than time machine. You can alter anything there in that universe, it won't change yours. You are safe either way. A child's play.'

'I get that now. But,see, parallel universe is not true. It's another unicorn.'

'Of course, this is a unicorn. But not from rainbows.'

'How can I trust you?'

'Not me. Trust the unicorn. Even if it's not true, it's harmless either.'

'Enlighten me,'he smirked.

'This helmet on the desk is called a **Universal Signal sender**. The **USR.** I'm going to mount this on your head and enter the requested data like time and date on this slim display called **vertical wall.** It'll collect the corresponding signal with all the data from your brain and along with some man made signals as catalyst and will hit the **Universal Signal Receiver, USV,** in **FLAME999**. The nearest satellite of sun. From there it'll get diffused in space and run in random until they find another sun. Which means another universe. Again doing an aribitary run, it'll reach the mind of your X with my navigation and your data. Then, the sneak, the swap,the switch whatever you call it.'

Mr.Cross exhaled heavily as the indication of his completion.

Calvry took the helmet in his hand. He rolled it up and side ways. Time machine,thought with a legal manslaughter,was a well-defined formula. But how could it be with this unrealistic diamond-in-the-sky tech. Of course, everyone loves to be an Alice in the wonderful. But what if the rabbit hole leads to the magical world dominated by deadly dragons? He let the mind go all the unrooted ways to get back. And, finally mounted the helmet on his head.

'I'm prepared to do it.'

He never failed to miss the jubilant spark in the eyes of Mr.Cross.

'We kick in then,' he jumped down from the desk and hit the power. The screen came to life. 'All set to go. And there's a limitation for this. You can't stay there for the whole day. This can give you only 10 minutes there. After that the signal will cut off automatically and you'll fall here.'

'Ten minutes? That's impressive,' he closed his eyes.

'Date and Time?'

'15th September, 2011. 16:15.'

'Don't sleep out, Calv. You are in safe glove,'he smiled a DOT52 smile,'What's special about the date actually?'

'Her birthday.'

Calvry went unconscious after that.

CHAPTER III

15 SEPTEMBER 2011

16:15

I feel a seductive nostalgia. I can smell a relief and revival. For the first time in my life I thank nerdy-baddy Cross for making this happen. This place, I'm sitting, could be cracked into two: BEFORE and AFTER her. Before I was into her, this was my war ground where everything's done in distractedly calm manner. After her, the war ground-the deadly depressing one- had suddenly blown into the sheets of handsome poetry. This day in this place twisted the entire dimension of my vertical red line. Now, I have only left ten minutes to shout and say that I love her. But, the mix-up I sense, this activity of me surely going to build her awkward and going to cut-off all the others around me. The basis for me to enter this exact time to avoid this and make her a warm room. It's ten minutes prior to the last bell for my language exam to end.

Being in this semi-day exam hall, my memories muscling me to bring a breeze to back of the body. Language is one the most exciting exams I love to take where I could scribble whatever I want to put some hefty score to my report. But I really hated when this exams were held at afternoon. Sleepy, long and bugging. I entered in with the sluggish and bored ideas that days. The hall was decent with long desks with both the corners and the middle space were numbered with choked chalks. I had my number written at the left corner of the second sitting. I yawned twice between the settling and the distribution of papers. That's the moment, it was staged. It made me little shittier to realize that one of my open mouth blow was bit louder. But, it was not that. I heard couple of knocks on my desk. I turned dull and it took me a family of sudden snaps to believe my own visionary. She was looking at me in my eyes, a stream of current, of course, and handed me two caramel candy.

It was her birthday. Instead of wishing her I thanked her. I never made any sense as I had no intention of approaching a girl even for the missed out geometry contents. This was fresh and damn a quake. My heartbeat vibrated my sticky hair strands through the earlobes. I was sure I have done nothing on purpose but spontaneously I turned to her side. First time. Then, second time. Believe. It's not me. Never. And, the third time. To the ground.

Though the day was hot, the wind was bit stormy. But that's OK. I detected the Chill at my back climbing to the neck almost freezing. she pressurized me to turn over and over. It was smooth when she was asking for extra sheets; otherwise I had to perform some circus tricks to turn towards her. No. It's not me again. She did that. She's responsible.

Her disobeying bunchy curly hair fell on her face, disturbing my view, aligned and tucked at the back of her ear. Her shiny piece of golden stud punched to her soft lobes glittered like hypnotic spiral. Her not-so-bright orange outfit, netted shawl and the connected bangle set,adjusted like dozen times, everything was perfect that day. May be the reason was her. She was colouring, moulding and scripting everything out-and-out precious. At the end of the session I know it's not going to end up here as she took over all the control.

I chose this place and situation because I wanted to dare myself to propose at the first sight. I need to believe in what the science have done to me. I see the parallel universe which is real, now. I'm at the exam hall with same season. Hot day, painy wind. Since, it's science, it's not so exact. I think I'm fucked.

The exam is not language; it's geography. And I'm sitting back of her when my seat is covered with a super handsome boy in the class. I touch my pocket, there's no candy. This universe is having other ideas for me, it seems. whatever it is my clock is ticking. I have to do something to have her attention.

'Excuse me,' I chest upon the desk and hissed. Calling her name, I fear, may create an abnormality and would collapse my motive by making me nervous. But I know this is the worst one.

She's still. no response.

The bunchy hair of her, teased my face with wind assistance. It's fragrant; that's dangerous.I bang my hand against the desk. I'm unstable.

I took my head to see around then to realize the spotlight is on me. The bang should had been louder than the usual.Her eyes are, too, on me now.

Her face conveyed no reaction. It's just sneaking into me like hundreds of javelin are pointing and poking all over me. Easy, easy, Easy. I asphyxiated. Stop that. I yell in silence.

'Happy birthday,' I whispered.

'Thank you,' she smiled. Limited but the razor-sharp one.

THANK YOU...THANK YOU....

My ears looped them in the partial deafness. She didn't moved her lips. Definitely not. But there're words I hear. She might have typed it to me. Typing a voice- a newer invention. My eyelids are heavy with tears.

'And..' My parched throat tried to pull out that. She tucked her hair behind and gave me a second. There's again this. THE GOLDEN EAR STUD. This is not occuring. I was hacked with pleasure codes.

'Yes.' Now I confirmed. Slight movement in words.'Oh,' she said and placed the caramel candy before me.

'Not this.' My parched words deepened. I was losing my vocabulary. I'm deliberately in needs of some words, now.

I gazed at her weak but straight. I need apologies for missing my sentences.

'Tell me,' she again. It gave me a whip of hope.

'I meant to,' I tried. But something is improper or I'm falling into a pit.

Everybody and all things around me suddenly begin to trip. My head was in the merry-go-round in all quick. I tried hard with my spirit to look at her but there was just her melted portion. The tears reservoired in my eyes started to pour. Nothing was there. All I see is a black and void.

My head hit strongly streaming a power migraine to suck my ability.

I woke up in the lab of cables and in front of Cross.

CHAPTER IV

'You didn't do it?'

Mr. Cross' eyeballs almost vacated the sockets.

'This is the most constructive and harmless way in the whole world to pull off your deliciously bizarre mission. But you say, you have failed it. Just like that.'

'I know that,'he limited, 'everything was a state-of-art to me and the milieu I have foreseen was in the fleshy shambles there. I'm just confused.'

'Is she was there?'

'Of course. I saw her in her eyes,' he sighed.

'Then, what? It was just a shout out. Nothing is going to change here. You could go home after that like nothing happened. And can continue yours. I didn't transfer you to some BRAVE NEW WORLD, did I?' Mr.Cross blistered.

'Not so simple as you say. Looks like you are much a hawkier than I,'he smirked.

'That's what I am. You are in my head now, Calv,'he exhaled, 'let's walk out of here. You killed this cat's curiosity,'

Mr.Cross sponged his face in the sandal soap water, wasted through the censored silver tap connected above the elite bath. The premium face dryer by the left did it's work to the core.He prepared himself for the scheduled next.

'There's a concert arranged in musicZ. Would you like to join? I'll cover your ticket. Don't say no. I'm getting you a official column.'

'No. Thank you.' Mr.Cross looked at him and found that he was unstable.

'You okay, Calv? Come on. You need this now,' he insisted.

'That wowey stuffs don't amuse me much nowadays. I can't stand with it. Getting to expire, you know. Falling old owns few rough edges too. I wanna go,'he sounded like a melodramatic tragedy.

'Then, I'll drop you home,' he said and sped to the elevator which opened on his arrival with the censor. He slid him inside and turned to press the call button. That's when he noticed Calvry was not there. Actually he was not following him the elevator. Mr.Cross,too,missed to cover his respond. 'Shit.'

He ran again to the desk they're in before.Number of ideas from his own crime fictions emerged and popped in head until he saw Calvry. Calvry was still standing near the desk, watching his phone seriously. Mr.Cross approached him in calm. At once ID'd the thing he was watching but not sure about the particular in the phone as the photography of a woman, no- a girl was bit slanting to his eyes. Calv put it back and acted naive.

'Hey, Calvy. You said you wanna go,' He almost mumbled.

'Yeah, I said I wanna go,' he smiled.

Mr.Cross sparked and sprang to the sky and back when he saw Calvry mounting the helmet like his mission off to mars. Of course it's afar than that.

'13 January 2016. 16:30.' Calvry closed his eyes.

'Thanks for taking my child's play seriously,' he winked.

13 January 2016

16:30

I'm gonna cook up a well-defined mess or a good story to escape from here. Last couple of years have taught me about fate, person and love. But confidence? Damn. In my speaking language confidence under lied as numbers. The mismatched entity. Above all, today I need that numerals more than I require.Though mastering them, anyway, have never been my mug of beer.

I was two hours earlier,now. To set myself for the legal encounter which is approved and signed by me. I was not hungry, not thirsty and even if you want to chop my toes off, I'd let you do that with a Godly grin. At least I could implant some distraction. I put on my earphones and turned on a classic song, staying in my playlist for years and got never played for years. But that mid-day, I admired it like my most favorite among the list. I tend to play it in loop. And I did it. My mind chewed up every word like every bit from my appetizing last meal. Like a surprising dessert in the middle of the meal the song abruptly allowed the phone to blare. It was a call for which I have been waiting for this long. The screen displayed her name.

'Hello.' I trapped my voice.

'I'm here. Where are you?' A no grand elegant voice.

'Near by private bus terminal.'

'Me too. But I couldn't see you.' She sounded sober.

I spun myself to see her at any corner as I know I reached her almost. Since it's a festival season whole bus terminal is pouring out.

I don't believe in anything magical or ghostly until it happened. Having no derived possibility of seeing her again I moved to a far away city to take my bachelor. The first year shifted like anything- no strict classes, no mathematics and science and more intriguing stories. I found myself in the safe and apt fit. But somewhere in me I regretted a pile of pain and wander for her. It was not her face or curvy figure but her presence. Just that. Sometimes I expected her to present in my class like the movie thing which is nearly a needle in the hay. Whenever I happen to see my old mates I collected the whereabouts and howabouts of the other classmates just to hear about her. Crazy idea still satisfying results. And, That's how I came know she's literally in my next city. Months flipped. Fortunately and startlingly, from one of my mate I registered her phone number. The recovered lost needle after setting the hay on fire. An exclusive hatch of the phone it was so easy to loud out your sentences. That's my ground too. We spoke and shared like a hell of things for the months. As like how it has to be termed, we decided to meet today. Fate, person and love- all the three fell in my hand like a magical wand which was my solid superstition.

I couldn't find her in the rush. I scootered to the whole platform from freezy north to breezy south. Still I fell short to get to her. I don't want to make her wait for me for this long. I was making it worse for me. **Don't hate me. I'll find you.**

She called me again which made me little scared. May be she was canceling the meet. May be next time. May be some reasonable alibis. I rehearsal her ground of the call without attending it. With no options left I picked up the call.

'Stay where you are. I got you,' she's still sober.

I stood still like a task installed fleshbot. She walked towards me from the other side of the platform. Damn I was searching in opposite. I felt a load of bricks on my shoulder, pushing to fall on the ground.

'How you doing?' she asked.

'Fine.' Nothing ran out officially.

'Let's find our bus and before that let's get something to eat,' she smiled.

'It's your treat. For you high points in last semester,' I said.
Behave. Don't be a cheap.

'I remember. You can load up anything you want.' That's adorable. Actually I was hungry now.

We shopped couple of LAYS spanish tomato tango, a SPRITE and a GOOD DAY choco chip cookies pack. I refuged a warmth with her. Honestly, it was she who made my pulse normal. I wanted to stay longer than scripted before. But the fate is avail in your pocket; you can't slip away. There was a bus with no rush. And I have another half-an-hour bonus.

Tearing off the LAYS pack, we sit near but not on the same seat. I held the packet in my hand and we begin to partake slowly. Chat about the comic incidents staged in college, derailed yet funny decisions of our schoolmates and some personals went in row. Whenever she dropped her hand inside the pack to pick the chips up, it was officially into mine on which she never bothered.

The pack was over and we shared the sprite too. I picked out my phone to check the time as I forgot to bring my watch.

'That's the interesting wall paper,' she said like a baby.

I handed the phone to her. **Nothing to hide. You have all the access.** *She went through my gallery and we made fun of some of the pictures. I had to admit it I couldn't screen myself before her even if wanted to. She handed the phone back. Then she unlocked her phone and gave it to me. Is this the payoff? Definitely not. This is thing that makes a boy a man. TRUST. She trusts me. I sensed that in her. I don't want to dig so deep.* **Behave.** *I just skimmed some of her not-so-filtered super cool pictures. Specifically, the picture of her where she was balancing a pillow in her head. It made me laugh and admire at the same time. Predominantly, she joined me. While handing the phone back we looked in our eyes for a second. An unadulterated blissful moment. Her phone blinked for the notification which featured the time on the main screen. 16:30. Perfect timing.*

While speaking about fate and love again, they play a twin sometimes. Jeopardizing the moments. When I planned a perfect timing for the proposal. This scientific helmet thing had other ideas. Dusted but true- the other side of the flipped coin.

This time, it's superbad and shuffled than before.

CHAPTER V

Literally, it took some least instants for me to understand what the half-drunk game I'm trying to force me in. Last time I almost to line, the border line. But, now, this is quite a heavy toxic portion. I'm still in the bus, jammed in the traffic. If this has to be carried out, it would take twenty minutes to reach the terminal as the traffic is already being a deep ocean. No motion or improvement, suspense and scary in parts. But I'm not going to crap out my minutes. I know what to do.

I stepped down from the bus that never seized an inch. I watch the vehicles arranged in a lopsided manner and honking to screw away the ears of previous one's driver. In front of the bus, there was brand new truck loaded with roof bricks and and navy green four wheeler with a friend state license plate. From the opposite side by the traffic light number of motor bikes ranged and racing with an illuminating purple bus stationed behind them blaring in frustration. I flashed to the immediate alley,a short cut, I used before. It'd take nearly ten minutes If I walk. But I'm not going to walk. No spring water walks. I run.

I sped like I'm expiring soon. Of course, it's a halfway Yes. I felt little light regardless of my huge shoulder bag teasing my butt like stuffed toy. I ran like a human turned monster flee to destroy the race in some darkly moneyed superhero movies. But this running time have cleaved my duration. I was soon as I thought. Crossing the number of aimlessly moving buses I reached to the platform. The right one. I have no minutes to bluff up. The bus we boarded was there in the platform. She must be in there. Waiting for me. I boarded in pushing myself. The final big piece. An exact bite. Except she's not there in the bus.

I took my phone off to notice five jumped calls from her. It should've hit my phone while running that I didn't focus on. I swiped her number and she picked up the call in couple of rings.

'I saw you,' the first word she told when the call is picked felt just like an scripted realism. Hit and miss.

'Where are you? I'm in the platform searching for you. You're not here,' I exploded.

'I'm sorry.'I hear her breathing heavily.

'What happened? Are we cool?,' I still hear her breathing. What the hell of the story with this universe?

'I got jammed up in the traffic and I saw you hoping out of bus and running through that alley. I saw you from the opposite side of the light.'

That purple bus. Smiled with an inside joke. Fuck.

'Where are you, now?'

'To your right.'

I turned like a sudden switch. I saw her walking towards me having her slim located backpack hugging her from behind. She was all sweaty and her loosened up fluffy hair trying to sponge it away.

'How... You?,' my tongue twisted.

'I followed you through the same alley,'she curved a beautiful a smile.

She has done exactly like I did. I smiled and laughed. She joined me in the same thoughts.

And, the picture melted away.

Calvry was clear-headed when he unmounted the helmet while Mr. Cross was drilling himself into Calvry's.

'What in the universe happened? Did you say her?.'

'Nope. But that's something of lovely perspective.'

'What's wrong with you? You're there just to say it.'

'As I said you before, it's not easy as that. Let's go for a coffee.'

'And?'

'We'll come back here for our next coordinate.'

'You think am I nuts? I'm running a machine to ensure this future. Not to dove or pigeon your love letters.'

'So?'

'So what that's it? I don't think you are here to do the thing you said. Spying on me rather, aren't you? For your shitty column worth no penny.'

Calvry rolled his eyes like a genius child and displayed a filled up form from his phone.

'I can see you recognize it. I changed my mind to apply for the time travel license. If you can help with this, I'll finish up the process. And, think of it what it makes if I do this.'

'Calvy, are you serious about this?'

'See by yourself.'

Mr.Cross flew to seize the phone and checked all away. His face came under a moonlight as bright as it can be.

'Coordinates, please.'

'Coffee, first.'

CHAPTER VI

18 JANUARY 2019
14:10

The last chance is always like a small yet delicious finale of the Cornetto. Treasury with much patient demand. So was this chance. I'm not gonna ask Mr.Cross another one. Because literally after this scene we're not going to be similar; everything has changed. A new diagram inside the same perimeter.

We haven't met each other for last three years. That's pretty long gap. In luck, our phone calls and texts rolled in uninterrupted. Most of them were sleek and sharp. Rarely, extensive, funny and pour outs. At that times, I begun to admire her laughter, slang, anger even the minor pause. But one thing I was sure in these days, we can not spare all our times in flirts and jokes. We're growing. Not the school kids anymore. We spear up with responsibilities. Though all my nights and happy moments required her to be in the present. I needed her literally. I inhaled lot of love in this silent undecipherable distance.

I'm going to see her today after the enough gap. And once again it jabbed back all the events and incidents we've gone through evenly. I predicted this day would come anyway.

Her sister's wedding.

Usually, I spoil the things when I accompany someone. So I preferred myself as a flawless company every time. Kind of should be for this turn. I never raced my two wheeler like I do always. I need to be slow and steady to avoid myself caught up in the situation. Making the clear sky grey. And, the other thing I cared about is the crowd and noise. I always hated me for being this sensitive. Try puncturing me with thread, you win.

I reached the wedding hall without any strain in finding it. Parked and keys off. To my analyse, it's set there welcoming to scare me. Mobbed and louder. Instead to locate things for myself I felt lost. I was short of assistance. I dialed her.

'I'm here,' I trembled nearly.

'Walk forward. I got you.' A freshness in her voice shouldered me enough. ***Why it should be you always to find me in the first place?***

There she was stated like a blue bird squeaking. Nothing is changed in her way. Rather I felt a completion with her. I suddenly able connect with her in person. Though the thing called love stirred me nervous, her person tied me safe. I adjusted my backpack to slant right.

'You put little weight, huh?' I had to start but not with this. Done what never had to be.

'Yeah,' she said like she never cared. She cared. Everyone does.

In sudden, I heard a high frequency ring from the loud speakers which made me squeeze the face. Playing psych. We stood there and talked very little like a warm up. About the man giving a wedding speech in the stage, I was introduced to her mother and the other starter talks. Again the speaker and psych me.

Finally, she walked me to the stage and I was introduced as friend to her sister. Powerful and witty. Then the photography ritual. While going down the stage the blocks of gifts were stacked in her hand. She balanced herself to save them from falling. While crossing the crowd she'd definitely drop at least two.

'You need a hand,' I volunteered and transferred some from her while she picked my backpack from the stage. We came down and landed the gifts on the safe place where the stacks

cannot be distrubed.

'Have something,' she navigated me to the dining hall. Though I hate being with mass I attended programs and functions for this single benefit. Feast. The only thing to capture my entire concentration. Another benefit I had that day, I could reserve some more minutes to spend with her again. That's much crucial. That was the exact time I received a call. It was her.

'Is everything OK out there?' She did what have to to be done. But for me it's peculiar.

'Yeah. fine here.'

'Feel free to eat.' I will. I would. Always.

The crowd had already started dissolving. By the time the dining hall begin to fill up as the most part of the dissolved begin to settle in there. We both stood facing each other to say bye. Chance of good byes are at high stake when I had no plans about that. We had our final talks before I walk. The whole conversation sensed like a figure of speech to ***'the end.'***

'So...'

I said in the meaning to extend the conversation for infinity. I needed her eyes to stagger me forever, our little talks to build a great towers, the remaining of life to unchain us and the suspension to be swallowed to save me from the heart attack.

This is the moment.

I chose this time not just this is the perfect whip to convey but I became a sudden chauvinist to prove my ability to do. Behalf of the acknowledgement what about to be happen I can do this with no second thought. Happily forever.

The universe concept not always pitiful. At least for this time everything is staged as it was. I met her as the blue bird, quirky beginning, loud embarrassment, photography ritual, volunteering to hand and the feasty benefit. Now, I'm here in front of her to finish the long running series.

'So...,'I started.

She followed the word to have a cloudy stare at me.

'So?,' she said sarcastically. I lubricated my lips to save me from the tangled utterance.

'Hey.'

I turned back and there was he. The charming super handsome boy from my class.

'Calvy?,' he widened his eyes, 'I never expected to meet you here.'

'Me too,' I pretend to act nice, 'How you doing?'

'I'm super fine,' he shot his flirty smile. Simultaneously, I looked at her. This universe is not parallel. It's pathetic.

She blushed.

'OK Calvy. Wait here, if you love to. I'll navigate Cross to the dining hall,' she winked and moved away with handsome Cross. Mr.Cross.

I should be waiting here. May be I have a chance. But my time won't. It has a faster melting point.

CHAPTER VII

DOT52 entered into the room holding a file in her arms and rested it on the table. Mr.Cross unlocked the screen of the file with his thumb impression and signed it with no inspection further. He let it rest there as it is. Calvry noticed the all-time-rumbling facial muscles of Mr.Cross being seen drained a little. The half-powdered cigarette was punched into smoke at the ground of the shining silver ashtray. Calvry was never invited for a smoke which's bit exceptional new twist.

'Your training license is signed. Join us from next week.' He mumbled, not looking at Calvry's face.

'Yeah. Sure,' he replied, 'Thank you.'

'Thank you? You see that, I have fucked half of my day just aiding you to say HI to your girlfriend from nowhere,' He erupted.

'At least you got a free run for your new invention.'

'Free run. I would have used a dog, monkey or any of humanoid to test that thing. Not you,' He lit another cigarette, ' I wanted to take a success ride on your mission. But, damn! You failed me, stupid. You see that.'

'If that's so... I drop myself for a apology.'

'Nope. That's not the exact way, I think. Not my way.'

'What do you expect then?.'

'Smart! Here comes my turn,' he grinned like a demon, 'I need to you to pour light on two of my questions. Least I could dig from you to sleep in peace.'

'Shoot. I'll try.'

'Exciting. First of first, what happened in there or why didn't you propose her?'

Calvry sighed. Breath of dinosaur. 'Have you ever been with a girl, Cross?'

'Yeah. I did. I'm not a happy-home-happy-family guy, obviously. But I have been with some girls before. Like livin' or a night stand type.'

'That's quite obvious, too. And, have you ever came up with the feelings for them?'

'What's the hell of question is this. Of course, I've been with girls and made love. You sounds nuts, Calvy.'

'Living with girls and having something organic...Both are not the same.'

'Enlighten me.'

'The thing of you which is actually not so is just like DOT52. Command, receive and discard. And my kind is the baby. It cries, shits, vomits but when you pamper, it'll make you blush.'

'Lunatic. Whatever, that never sounds like my answer.'

'On my thought, I put forward three things that stopped me. When I prepared myself to say words for first I was in need of tons of hours to consume the bridge between us that's pale. It's all because of Love. Saintly love.'

' HA..HA...saintly!Then?'

'When I was at the bus terminal, already acquired a better acquaintance, the scenario was ruined by fate. It held the thing back. For the third time, all together it was her.'

'How come her?'

'That's our meeting after a long time. I sensed a maturity in there struggling and it butted me back to the first like a cycle. That's when I realized I'm still at the beginning. And some external peer pressure.'

'I don't get it. But I'm convinced,'

'Stop loving DOT52. You'll be able to cover the syllabus.'

'The second question...when we started I had no profit from you getting me a disclosure on this. I thought it was none of my shitty business and I need to be a boy of excel in all criteria. But after all this I'm graving to know this. Who is that girl?'

Calvry busted into laughter. 'It's Anri.'

Mr.Cross' jaw dropped and his facials snapped in a second.

'What the hell is this Calvy? You are a pig. The insane pig I ever know. If it was her, then why me? Why my idea to stage that? You made my day a living hell. If this is what you say love, I'd name it as a crap. Go home before I call Anri to say what you are and what's your motive.'

'That's not the deal.'

'There's no deal. Get your face out of me.'

Calvy got himself out of the room, managing to intake his laughter.

CHAPTER VIII

That night was bright as the day. The cold moon light kept seducing the leaves on the trees to have a secret convo. Though it's not so late, the place was calm and soothing. Calvry walked through the way, filling his ears with the oozing wind and faraway city's rocks. He walked alone and that never spooked him anyway. Sometimes he prefers to sit at the stone benches by the way to enjoy his sky time. But that night he paced straight to home.

The moonlight haven't left the lonely wooden house either. When Calvry see that he smiled to himself. He followed the darkness dropped like the old particles of sky to the pebbles branded door way and knocked it twice.

May be wacky it is. He was cent percent sure, Mr. Cross not going to hit a peace sack tonight. Robots don't bleed. But the preaching on those three things and the Anri thing should have brain damaged him.

He swirled his life back for a minute to get a crystal view about the beast. The fourth thing. Might be it was love, fate and person which runs or stops the human race. But there's another finest one which wheels all the three- the destiny.

Calvry heard the door unlocking. At once, his all inclusive philosophical intuition flew away. It's time to face the destiny. Anri opened the door and put a smile to her wrangled chin.

'Where you been all the day. I was worried,' she forced to look at him when he detached from her.

'I was just outside. Hunting for news.'

'You should've told me. I was at the phone for the whole day expecting your call.'

'I was occupied. As I said so.'

'Come. Let's eat.'

'I'm not hungry. I need to sleep.'

'Still angry, right?'

'No not all. I'm just tired.'

Anri caught his arms tightly and begun to sob, burying her face on his chest.

'I'm sorry. I went mad. I never meant anything I said in the morning. I behaved a fool. You don't have to prove yourself in the past. That doesn't matter for me. But please don't punish me with this.'

'Hey listen. I'm not angry at all,' he took her face in his hands and charmed a kiss on her forehead,'I'm not angry. Just nervous. You know the thing I always wanted to say to you?'

Anri remained silent nodding her head like a baby. Allowing him to continue.

'You always been a stunner. And I'm your big fan.'

Anri smiled as he put her back to his chest. On the wall, in the photo shifting LED screen, a wedding picture was displayed. Anri in her butterfly white gown and Calvry in his firm blazer.

19 JANUARY 2019

14:15

In half heart I turned towards the gate with an improper farewell. My throat stoned like a reservoir saving a dam to explode. I looked back twice. She's standing at the same place gazing at my way.

'Calvy.'

I heard her. It almost fainted my cards.

'Say it.'

'What?'

'Spit it Calvy. No more stay.'

Tear drops rolled down without any approval. And she blushed to the ground and moon which reddened her clear cheeks.

9 798889 865896

Printed by Libri Plureos GmbH in Hamburg, Germany